A Musical Journey

From the Great Wall of China
to the Water Towns of Jiangnan

Created and Written by
Liow Kah Joon

SilkRoad™

Published by SilkRoad Networks Inc. 2004

P.O Box 25072,
50 Boulevard Taschereau, Place La Citière,
La Prairie, J5R 5H4,
Québec, Canada

Website: **www.silkroad-childbook.com**

National Library of Canada Cataloguing in Publication Data

Liow, Kah Joon, 1970-
A musical journey : from the Great Wall of China to the water towns of Jiangnan /
by Liow Kah Joon.

Includes CD with original folk music.

ISBN 0-9733492-1-2

1. China—Description and travel—Juvenile literature. 2. China Civilization—
Juvenile literature. 3. China—Social life and customs—Juvenile literature.
4. Folk music—China. I. Title.

DS706.L56 2004   j951   C2003-907157-X

Music: cat_dog1234567
Art and Design: Wang Qun
English Text Editor: Tess Johnston
Research: Helen Jiang

Printed in Hong Kong

J172,784 E22

Introduction

In many ways, A Musical Journey has been my own journey.

I grew up as a third-generation Chinese in Singapore, speaking English as my first language. In 1998, I left Singapore to work and live in Shanghai, China. There, I rediscovered a culture into which I was born but paid scant attention to growing up in Singapore. My passable Chinese -- a source of amusement for my friends -- quickly gained fluency (and approving nods).

Three years later, I left my corporate job to pursue my interests. The rapid changes in Shanghai continued to hold my attention and I traveled frequently to the city in search of ideas. A Musical Journey was born in 2002 on one of these trips.

It started out as an idea to compose music for children. There are many families in North America who have adopted Chinese children. I know friends who have adopted one, two and even three Chinese girls. Through music, these families can experience the diverse land and people of their child's country.

Twelve musical themes were chosen and the rest of the book evolved from there. Some of the music is adapted from old folk songs of China. Most are original compositions. In each case we strived to make the arrangement fresh and appealing.

A highlight of the book is the illustrations of Ming and Kim, the two child guides, dressed in costumes of minority tribes. They are the visual representation of the music.

A Musical Journey is accompanied by a website, where additional fun and educational material can be found. Check it out at www.silkroad-childbook.com.

A second children's book is already in the works and is slated for publication in 2004.

Liow Kah Joon
December 2003
Montreal, Canada

Silk Road

Xinjiang

Great Wall of China

Tibet

Sichuan

Guizhou

Yunnan

Guilin

Great Wall of China

When seen from above the Great Wall looks like a dragon zigzagging over mountain tops. The Chinese call it "Wan Li Chang Cheng" which means "Wall of 10,000 Li". (10,000 li= 5,000 km)

Actually, the Great Wall is 7,200 km long. Height wise, it is 4.5m to 9m. Depth wise, it is 4.5m to 8m. The entire structure was built by hand using stone, bricks, soil, sand, straw, wood, clay or whatever was available depending on the terrain.

Three main Chinese dynasties — the Qin (B.C 221-207), Han (B.C 206-A.D 220) and Ming (A.D 1368-1644) — built the Great Wall. All had one purpose -- to keep out the "barbaric" Huns in the north who frequently invaded Chinese border areas. In all, tens of millions of people labored on the Great Wall. Many died.

Qin Shi Huang, the First Emperor of China, is credited with kicking off this massive project 2,200 years ago. By connecting old sections with newly built ones, the Qin Dynasty erected 4,800km of wall in 10 years – more than one km a day!

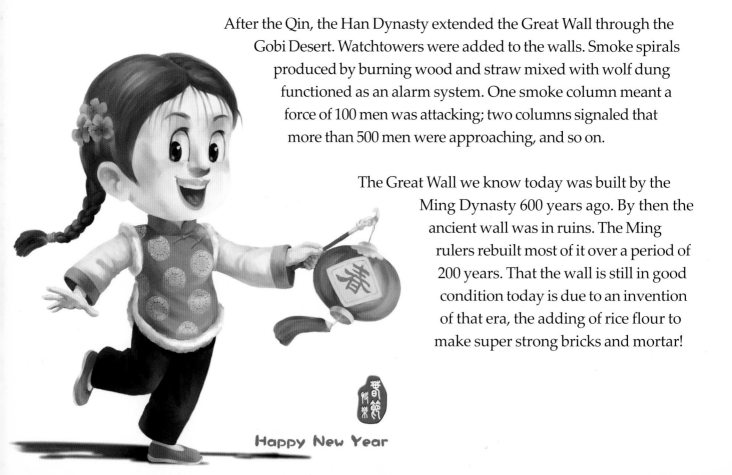

After the Qin, the Han Dynasty extended the Great Wall through the Gobi Desert. Watchtowers were added to the walls. Smoke spirals produced by burning wood and straw mixed with wolf dung functioned as an alarm system. One smoke column meant a force of 100 men was attacking; two columns signaled that more than 500 men were approaching, and so on.

The Great Wall we know today was built by the Ming Dynasty 600 years ago. By then the ancient wall was in ruins. The Ming rulers rebuilt most of it over a period of 200 years. That the wall is still in good condition today is due to an invention of that era, the adding of rice flour to make super strong bricks and mortar!

Happy New Year

Great Wall 万里长城

Silk Road

The Silk Road is a series of caravan routes which connected China and Europe some 2,000 years ago. Along these paths the exchange of ideas and inventions between East and West changed the world forever. In the 19ᵗʰ century, the name Silk Road was given to these historical trails by a German geographer, Ferdinand von Richthofen.

Paper, printing, gunpowder and the compass — the Four Great Inventions of China — reached the West through the Silk Road. Buddhism, one of China's three teachings along with Confucianism and Taoism, was imported from India through the Silk Road.

In China the Silk Road began in the Chinese capital Changan (modern-day Xian) in Shaanxi province and passed through Gansu province and Xinjiang Autonomous Region. In the Middle East it crossed Iran, Iraq and Syria before reaching the Mediterranean Sea.

Trade flourished in the oasis towns where caravans stopped to refill supplies. Buying and selling was carried out by a chain of middlemen. Going west, the Chinese traded with the Persians who dealt with the Syrians who did business with the Greeks who supplied the Romans.

The Roman nobles loved to wear clothes made of silk and paid a hefty price for the exotic fabric – in gold! Then only the Chinese knew how to produce silk. The Romans called the Chinese "silk people".

Other than silk, furs, ceramics, jade, bronze and lacquer objects, horses, gold, gems, perfumes, spices, dyes and textiles were traded on the Silk Road.

About 600 years ago, as sea trade became popular, the Silk Road declined, leaving behind a rich legacy.

Light of Wisdom

Silk Road 丝绸之路

Inner Mongolia

Inner Mongolia is in northern China. Steppes make up two-thirds of its terrain. A severe climate dominates the land. Winters are long and cold, rainfall is low and droughts are frequent.

The grasslands of Inner Mongolia are beautiful: Under blue skies, sheep and goats graze, and horses gallop across the plains.

Mongolians are skillful horse riders. The horse is a Mongolian's best friend.

A uniquely Mongolian musical instrument is the horse head fiddle. When played, it sounds like a horse neighing. The strings are made of horse hair. The handle is made of horse ribs.

Nadamu, an 800-year-old Mongolian tradition celebrating harvest season, is the biggest event of the year. There are horse races, roping competitions, archery and wrestling contests, and feasts of mutton eaten by hand. Mongolians do not eat fish because they believe fish is the food of the Gods.

Mongolians are a nomadic people. They needed a home that was light, portable and easy to assemble. This led to the development of the yurt. A yurt can be assembled in 2-3 hours.

Genghis Khan may be the most famous Mongolian in the world. The warrior was given the title "Emperor of Emperors" in 1206 after he united the people of the prairie in a series of military campaigns. At its peak, the Mongolian empire stretched from Hungary to Korea. It was the largest land empire in human history.

Spirit of Horse Rider

Grassland 草原

Xinjiang

Xinjiang Uyghur Autonomous Region is the largest of China's provinces and autonomous regions. Its terrain is a mix of mountains, basins, deserts, oases, and rivers.

Here, one will find the world's second highest peak, Mount Qiaogeli at 8,611 meters, and the second lowest place, Lake Aydingkol in the Turpan Basin at 154m below sea level. There is also the Taklamakan Desert — the second largest desert in the world. (Taklamakan means "he who goes in will not come out".)

Underneath the Turpan Basin is the Karez irrigation system. This is a manmade network of underground wells and canals which brings water from melted snow in the Tian Shan Mountains to the farmland in the valleys. As a result the scorching Turpan Basin is rich in grapes, Hami melons, and long staple cotton.

Most of Xinjiang's inhabitants are of the Uyghur tribe. An Islamic people, they speak Uyghur and write in an Arabic script. Uyghurs have a rich tradition of story telling, music and dance. All the Uyghurs — men and women, old and young — are fond of dancing, especially on holidays, festivals and wedding ceremonies. Their dancing is elegant and full of twirling movements of the head and hands.

Xinjiang food consists of roast mutton, kebabs, roasted fish, bread and rice, all eaten with the hand.

Dancing Queen

Grapes 葡萄

Tibet

Tibet Autonomous Region is situated on the Qinghai-Tibet plateau, the highest in the world, at an average elevation of 4,000m above sea level.

Tibet is surrounded by snow-capped mountains on all sides. In the south, the Himalaya Mountains are home to the highest peak in the world, Mount Everest, which stands at 8848m. Tibetans call Mount Everest "Mother Goddess of the Earth".

The life of the Tibetan people revolves around religion. The majority embrace Tibetan Buddhism, commonly called Lamaism. Lama means "teacher". At an early age, boys join the monasteries to be educated by Lamas. From these senior monks, they learn about Buddhism, and how to read and write, calculate, and meditate.

Sitting against the top of the Red Hill in Lhasa city is the monastery-like Potala Palace. About 1,300 years ago, Tibetan king Songtsen Gampo built the palace for his Chinese bride, Princess Wencheng of the Tang Dynasty.

The Potala Palace is comprised of the White Palace and Red Palace. These are the centers for political (white) and religious (red) affairs in old Tibet. Within the Potala Palace are more than 200,000 Buddhist statues of various sizes made of copper, silver or gold. Buried in the Red Palace are the tombs of past Dalai Lamas.

In Tibet, presenting a "kartha" to another person is a custom which shows sincerity and respect. A kartha is a white silk scarf. White is one of the three religious colors, along with red and yellow.

Eagle of Highland

Potala Palace　布达拉宫

Sichuan

One of the reasons Sichuan (Four Rivers) is called the Land of Abundance is because its plains are rich with crops all year round. More than 600,000 hectares of farmland receive water from the unique Dujiangyan irrigation project, developed 2,200 years ago.

Then Sichuan Governor Li Bin and his son found a way to harness the Minjiang River by dividing the water in two and channeling it. This practical and reliable method has spared Sichuan from droughts and famines for the last 2,000 years and is still in use today!

Giant pandas live in the Wolong Nature Reserve in Sichuan. Only 1,000 giant pandas are left in the wild. This black and white bear lives in the mountains and eats bamboo. It is a gentle animal and does not attack human beings or other animals.

In Leshan, the 71m tall Giant Buddha awaits. This is the largest Buddha in the world. It was carved into a cliff overlooking the intersection of three rivers 1,200 years ago. Completing the sculpture took all of 90 years.

There is a fairytale land in Sichuan called Jiuzhaigou (Nine Village Valley). It is a stunningly beautiful valley of lakes, waterfalls, snowy mountains and lush green forests. The myriad lakes are astonishingly colorful and crystal clear all the way down to 30m.

Sichuan has many minority tribes. The Yi tribe is the biggest with a population of one million. In the "Torch Festival" the tribe's people plant torches along field ridges and gather around bonfires drinking, singing and dancing through the night to pray for a good harvest.

Sichuan is famous for its fiery and tongue-numbing dishes. Lots of chili, red peppers and garlic are used in Sichuan food.

Prince of Music

Leshan Buddha 乐山大佛

Guizhou

Guizhou (Precious State) is an area of rich folk cultures blended into a natural landscape of waterfalls, limestone mountains and caves.

The largest waterfall in Asia, Huangguoshu (Yellow Fruit Tree) Waterfall, is found in Guizhou. At 68m high and 84m wide, it is a spectacular display of plunging water and arching rainbows.

Guizhou's "King of all Caves", Zhijin (Purple Gold) Cave, is filled with gigantic stalagmites and stone pillars of unusual shapes. Measuring 10km long, 150m high and 173m at its widest, the enormous cave features more than 40 types of limestone formations.

Fifteen ethnic tribes live in Guizhou, including the Miao, Yao, Dong, Buyi, Yi, and Shui. The Miao are the most colorful of all minority tribes in China for their dress and rituals. On festive occasions, such as harvest celebrations, Miao women wear lots of silver jewelry and silver headdresses. Each woman easily carries more than 10kgs of silver!

Like other tribes, Miao people enjoy singing and dancing. Their favorite musical instrument is the lusheng, a reed-type wind instrument. In a traditional lusheng dance up to thousands of dancers playing lushengs perform together, creating an awesome racket!

Batik technique is a folk art passed down through generations of the Miao and dates back more than 1,000 years. A pattern of flowers, birds, or fish is first drawn on white cloth with a knife dipped in hot wax. The cloth is boiled in indigo dye. After the wax melts, it leaves a white pattern on a blue background. One never knows what kind of pattern will finally appear. Therein lays batik's uniqueness.

Echoes in
the Mountains

Huangguoshu Waterfall 黄果树瀑布

Guilin

The city of Guilin lies on the Li River in the Guangxi (Vast Land in the West) Autonomous Region. Guilin means "Forest of Osmanthus Trees". The name is derived from the osmanthus trees found all over the city.

Guilin lies in a land of bizarre peaks, strange caves and misty rivers. Every scene is a classical Chinese landscape painting brought to life. For ages Guilin has been the source of inspiration for artists and poets in China. These ancients have given Guilin the title "Best Scenery under Heaven".

The peaks have imaginative names such as "Town of Strange Pinnacles", Wave Curbing Hill", "Solitary Beauty Peak", and "Folded Brocade Hill".

Elephant Trunk Hill is the best known of Guilin's peaks. The rock hill with an arched hole, at the junction of the Li and Yang rivers, is so called because it looks like an elephant drinking water.

Fubo (Wave Curbing) Hill is another interesting sight. Half the hill is in the river and the other half on land. At the base of Fubo Hill is the Huanzhu (Returned Pearl) Cave which is filled with Buddhist statues and wall scriptures. According to legend the cave was once inhabited by a dragon guarding a pearl. A fisherman stole the pearl but later, stricken by shame, he returned it to the cave.

Reed Flute Cave is the largest and grandest cave in Guilin. It is 240m deep and contains marvelous formations of stalactites, stalagmites, and stones. It is said the reeds growing by the cave's mouth could be made into flutes. That is how the cave got its name.

Picking Tea Leaves

Fishing 捕鱼

Yunnan

Yunnan means "South of the Colorful Clouds". Legend has it that 2,000 years ago the emperor saw rosy clouds in the southern skies and sent scouts to search for the source. The area where the clouds appeared was renamed Yunnan.

Yunnan is mostly mountains. In the northwest, Yunnan borders on the Himalayas. This region has the mildest climate (average temperature 8 to 20 degree Celsius) in China and plenty of plants and flowers. Hence Yunnan's nickname "Land of Eternal Spring".

Yunnan has the largest number of minority tribes — 26 — in China. They include the Bai, Yi, Miao, Dai and Naxi.

__The Golden Peacock is the symbol of Yunnan.__ It is found in southern Yunnan in the forests of Xishuangbanna, home to the Dai tribe. Many wild animals long extinct in other parts of China, such as tigers, elephants, and rare birds, can be found in Xishuangbanna.

The Dai live in houses built on stilts. In mid-April each year they celebrate the New Year by splashing water on each other during the Water Festival.

The old town of Dali in northwestern Yunnan is the home of the Bai people. For 1,000 years the Bai have been making tie-dye cloth. This cloth is blue with lovely white patterns. It is made by soaking cloth sewn with thick knots in indigo dye.

Each year at the Butterfly Spring thousands of colorful butterflies hang on the branches of an ancient tree that hangs over the water. Legend has it that a pair of lovers turned into butterflies, rose from the spring and flew away happily. Bai boys and girls come to the Butterfly Spring to celebrate their courtship.

Peacock Princess

Xishuangbanna 西双版纳

Dongbei

Dongbei (Northeast) is comprised of Jilin, Liaoning and Heilongjiang provinces. It is a bitterly cold region.

Dongbei people are known for their hearty nature and ability to consume great amounts of alcohol.

Large tracts of fertile black soil make up the plains. Dense forested mountains supply plenty of timber. Ample reserves of petroleum, coal and iron are extracted from the ground.

Foreign conquerors have always been drawn to Dongbei's rich resources.

China's last dynasty, the Qing Dynasty (1644-1911), was ruled by the Manchus. The Manchus set up their capital in Shenyang (now capital of Liaoning). Dongbei was called Manchuria.

After the Qing Dynasty collapsed the Japanese moved in. From 1932-1945, Changchun was the capital of Japanese Manchukuo. Puyi, the deposed last emperor of China, was installed as a puppet ruler by the Japanese.

Harbin (capital of Heilongjiang) was created in the 1890s when the Chinese government allowed Russia to build a railway in China. Harbin was in every way a Russian city. Today, many Orthodox churches line the streets of Harbin.

In Harbin, ice sculpting is a popular activity in winter. Human figures, dragons and pagodas are hacked from ice blocks in temperatures down to -38 degree Celsius!

Yang Ge Boy

Little Inn 小客栈

Central Plains

Some 4,000 years ago, Chinese civilization was born in the lower Yellow River basin in Henan province and spread outwards. Known as Zhong Yuan (Central Plains), this region includes present day Shanxi, Shaanxi, Shandong, Hunan and Hubei provinces.

Shaolin Temple is the cradle of Chan (Zen) Buddhism and Shaolin martial arts in China. Founded 1,500 years ago, Shaolin Temple is located in the forests of Songshan Mountain in Henan province. Shaolin means "New Forest".

According to legend, an Indian monk, Bodhidharma, taught the Shaolin monks martial arts to toughen them up for the rigors of Buddhist study. Using these fighting skills, the monks defended the temple against bandits.

In Shaolin history, the most famous story is about 13 fighting monks who saved the Tang emperor (1,300 years ago) from an invading army. Shaolin Temple was rewarded handsomely by the emperor. A corps of warrior monks who served the emperor came into being.

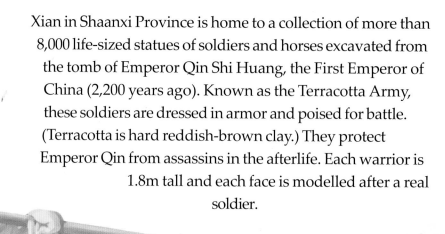

Xian in Shaanxi Province is home to a collection of more than 8,000 life-sized statues of soldiers and horses excavated from the tomb of Emperor Qin Shi Huang, the First Emperor of China (2,200 years ago). Known as the Terracotta Army, these soldiers are dressed in armor and poised for battle. (Terracotta is hard reddish-brown clay.) They protect Emperor Qin from assassins in the afterlife. Each warrior is 1.8m tall and each face is modelled after a real soldier.

Construction of the massive tomb complex began when Emperor Qin ascended the throne at age 13. Some 700,000 forced laborers worked for 35 years to complete it. (Emperor Qin was building the Great Wall at the same time!)

Shaolin Kid

Yellow River 黄河

Jiangnan

Jiangnan means "South of the Yangtze River". At 6,300km, the Yangtze is the longest river in China.

Jiangnan includes Jiangsu, Zhejiang, and Anhui provinces. Through the ages Jiangnan has been the wealthiest region in China, producing first-rate rice, silk and tea leaves.

Jiangnan is famed for its scenic water towns and lakes. A typical water town is Zhouzhuang. This 900-year-old town has arched bridges, winding streams and quaint houses in the old Chinese style. Among the lakes, West Lake (Xihu) and Tai Lake (Taihu) are the most beautiful.

Jiangnan's natural beauty is captured in the Chinese saying "Paradise in Heaven, Suzhou and Hangzhou on Earth".

Suzhou is a 2,500 year-old city known for its silk and its bamboo gardens. Everything about Suzhou, starting from its spoken dialect, is like a feminine Chinese beauty: soft, subtle and elegant.

West Lake lies in the west of Hangzhou, hence its name. Poets, writers and artists have been inspired by West Lake for centuries. Names such as "Three Pools Mirroring the Moon", "Viewing Fish at Flower Harbor" and "Autumn Moon on Calm Lake" describe the beauty spots along West Lake.

The mountains surrounding West Lake produce Longjing (Dragon Well), an excellent green tea. Early in April each year the best Longjing tea leaves are harvested.

Pretty Jade

Suzhou Garden 苏州

New Folk Music

Chinese Drum

1. Great Wall of China -- The Chinese Dragon

A lion dance is performed on the Great Wall during Chinese New Year celebrations. Chinese drums and cymbals convey a feeling of happiness. This is an adaptation of music played during festive occasions.

2. Silk Road -- Connecting East and West

Central Asian traders on camels laden with treasures brave the Taklamakan Desert to reach China. Foot bells and the tambourine are featured in this original composition.

Tambourine

Horse Head Fiddle

3. Inner Mongolia -- Flying across the Grasslands

A Mongolian rider on horseback is racing across the plains. This composition uses elements of traditional Mongolian music and features the horse head fiddle.

4. Xinjiang -- Land of Song and Dance

A young Uyghur girl dances at a festive occasion. Sounds of the rawap feature mainly in this composition.

Rawap

Bamboo Flute

5. Tibet -- Roof of the World

Tibetan boys and girls are celebrating. This is an original musical piece with bamboo flute and Tibetan drum and banjo.

6. Sichuan -- Land of Abundance

This updated folk melody paints a scene of Yi people singing and dancing around a bonfire to celebrate a good harvest. Its distinctive sound is made by a bawu, a type of Chinese clarinet.

Bawu

Lusheng

7. Guizhou -- Land of Color

Miao people relay messages, including expressions of friendship and love, to each other through song. These songs echo through the mountain ranges. A Miao girl plays the lusheng.

8. Guilin -- Best Scenery under Heaven

This tune depicts the young women of Guangxi's Zhuang tribe picking tea leaves in the spring morning sun. In the background are the beats of copper drums.

Copper Drum

Wooden Drum

9. Yunnan -- Land of Eternal Spring

The bamboo dance is a popular dance among the minority tribes of Yunnan. Dancers move deftly between bamboo poles accompanied by the rhythmic beats of copper and wooden drums.

10. Dongbei -- The Cold North

This cheerful music, known as Yang Ge, is played by performers in street parades during festive celebrations. Thousands of spectators line the streets. The main instruments are the banhu, erhu, Chinese drums and cymbals.

Banhu

Pipa

11. Central Plains -- Cradle of Chinese Civilization

Under a tree, a grandfather plays a small bamboo flute while a little boy chases a small bird around the tree. The bamboo flute imitates a bird singing. Another main instrument is the pipa. This is an original composition.

12. Jiangnan -- Heaven on Earth

This is a new version of Jasmine Flower, a 200-year-old Jiangnan folk song. Erhu and pipa are the main instruments. Jasmine is a small, white, sweet-scented flower. One imagines sitting in a boat rowing down the canal in Zhouzhuang, passing under arched bridges with old houses on both banks.

Erhu

To Be
Continued . . .